KU-014-077

RACCOON RAMPAGE
THE RAID

ANDREW COPE

Illustrated by Nadia Shireen

HarperCollins *Children's Books*

First published in Great Britain by
HarperCollins *Children's Books* 2012
HarperCollins *Children's Books* is a division of
HarperCollins*Publishers* Ltd, 77-85 Fulham Palace Road,
Hammersmith, London W6 8JB

Visit us on the web at
www.harpercollins.co.uk

1

Raccoon Rampage: The Raid
Text copyright © Andrew Cope 2012
Illustrations copyright © Nadia Shireen 2012

Andrew Cope and Nadia Shireen assert the moral right to be
identified as the author and illustrator of this work.

ISBN 978-0-00-746266-7

Printed and bound in England by
Clays Ltd, St Ives plc

Conditions of Sale
This book is sold subject to the condition that it shall not, by way of
trade or otherwise, be lent, re-sold, hired out or otherwise circulated
without the publisher's prior written consent in any form of binding
or cover other than that in which it is published and without a
similar condition including this condition being imposed on the
subsequent purchaser.

MIX
Paper from
responsible sources
FSC
www.fsc.org
FSC C007454

FSC™ is a non-profit international organisation established to promote
the responsible management of the world's forests. Products carrying the
FSC label are independently certified to assure consumers that they come
from forests that are managed to meet the social, economic and
ecological needs of present and future generations,
and other controlled sources.

Find out more about HarperCollins and the environment at
www.harpercollins.co.uk/green

Dedication

For Lou.

About time you got a mention!

CHAPTER 1

The Rules

The trees were heavy with snow. Clouds scudded across the night sky and an owl hooted. The Hole-in-the-Tree gang scampered through the forest, heading for the twinkling lights of the village. Rocky's teeth were chattering, a combination of cold and fear. "What if he's waiting for us?" he panted. "Max isn't stupid. And he's got a gun. I've heard he kills animals and stuffs them. And then keeps them in his house to look at." Rocky's teeth started chattering even faster. "He looks at d—dead animals! For fun!"

Quickpaw stopped abruptly and pulled his team into the moonlight. He put a paw across Rocky's mouth. "Shush," he ordered. "We need cool raccoon heads. Max knows we're coming. We've seen him setting traps." Rocky's eyes widened and he let out a muffled shriek. "That's why we're going with Sunshine's plan," explained Quickpaw. "He's the most cunning raccoon in the forest. He is an expert at breaking and entering. Has there ever been a job too difficult for our light-fingered friend?"

All eyes fell on Sunshine. His half-tail was a souvenir of a previous mission that had gone horribly wrong. He carefully raised the brim of his cowboy hat and cast a glance at the gang. "Ain't nothin' that this outlaw can't break into," he said, sounding more confident than he felt.

"And what exactly is your plan?" asked Dempsey. "I sure am hungry. But Rocky's right, Max is on red alert. How on earth are we going to break into his shop?"

The Sunshine Cub stood tall, meerkat-style. "Max is expecting us to break into his shop. Right?"

"Right," chorused the gang.

"Which is exactly why we're *not* going to break into his shop."

The other raccoons looked at Sunshine in puzzlement. "We're not?"

"Rule number one of breaking and entering: hit 'em by surprise."

Rocky tugged nervously at the elastic in his pants. He didn't like surprises.

"It's winter, right?" continued Sunshine. "All this cold white stuff means food is scarce. And the lake is frozen. And Max knows that us hungry critters will do anything to get our hands on his food. So I cased the joint yesterday." Dempsey looked puzzled. "Did a bit of snooping," explained Sunshine. He moved to a clear bit of snow and drew a map of Max's General Store with his paw. The gang huddled round the moonlit diagram. "Traps at the front door," explained

Sunshine, putting a cross in the snow. More crosses followed. "Traps on the top shelf next to the gherkins. Poison next to the oatmeal. And a newly installed guard dog sleeping in a basket behind the counter."

Rocky couldn't take much more. "P—p—poison? And a d—d…"

Sunshine barged on. "So we're not going to go anywhere near where Max expects us to be. That'd be curtains for the Hole-in-the-Tree gang. Our last supper! No siree." He drew another box on the side of Max's shop. "That's why we're going to break into Max's storeroom."

There was a collective sharp intake of racoon breath. "The storeroom!" echoed Rocky. "Nobody's ever broken into Max's secret store!"

Dempsey sat upright. "I saw in there once," he drooled. "Loads and loads of fish, in a cold cupboard. And enough packets of biscuits to last a raccoon lifetime."

"I saw it too," moaned Rocky. "It's raccoon suicide. Not only is the storeroom *inside* the shop, but there are padlocks everywhere. There's a good reason why animals have never broken into the storeroom. We'll never get through the door!"

"Who said anything about going in through the door?" beamed Sunshine, cocking his hat and raising an eyebrow. "Rule number two of breaking and entering: be creative. Humans would call it 'thinking outside the box'." His friends stared at him expectantly. "The storeroom has one door, padlocked and bolted, right?"

The gang nodded. "And no windows," added Dempsey.

"Exactly!" exclaimed Sunshine. He paused to take in their blank faces. "Don't you see? No windows? If there are no windows then Max isn't going to expect a break-in through a window."

Dempsey scratched his ear. He could feel one of his headaches coming on. Rocky blinked hard. Even Quickpaw was struggling to keep up.

"So we *make* a window," continued Sunshine. "Rule number three: expect the unexpected. And tonight is the perrrrfect night for the unexpected."

The other three raccoons listened intently. The moon disappeared and the forest went black. Sunshine had an excellent breaking-and-entering record, but this seemed an impossible raid. "There's been a posse of workmen in town. Making a crazy racket! Digging up the roads and laying cables." The raccoon removed his hat and felt for his camera. He'd stolen it from a tourist a few months ago and it was his favourite gadget. He clicked it on and the gang crowded round to marvel at the saved pictures. There were several men in luminous jackets, some with huge drills and one driving a digger.

"So we're going in through the tunnels..." guessed Dempsey, jumping up and down with excitement.

"An interesting idea," nodded Sunshine. "But no." He looked around as if somebody might be listening, and drew the gang closer. "I enlisted the help of Headbanger and he's been working on our behalf."

"Headbanger?" chorused the gang. "The woodpecker?"

"We've taken advantage of the noise. While the drill's been drilling, Headbanger's been pecking. Nobody saw him and, more importantly, nobody heard him."

Sunshine led the raccoons across the empty road and they scampered through the shadows towards Max's General Store. They tiptoed past the front door, being careful not to wake the dog. Sunshine unfolded a piece of paper that he'd been carrying and studied it.

The gang watched as he stood at the corner of Max's shop and marched ten extra-large raccoon paces, leaving tiny footprints in the snow. He stopped abruptly and beckoned to his friends.

"Rocky, you're the lightest. Get on my shoulders." Rocky didn't look sure, but he was helped aboard by Dempsey and Quickpaw. Sunshine turned to face the wooden wall of Max's storeroom. "Headbanger should have cut a circle," he barked. "Loosened the wood. Hit it, right there in front of your face and we're in."

Rocky looked down at his friends. He turned back to the wooden wall, formed a fist and thumped as hard as he could. Sure enough, a small circle of wood disappeared, clattering on to the floor inside Max's storeroom. The gang tensed, waiting for the dog to bark. There was no sound so Rocky peered into the hole. His keen raccoon eyes picked out rows and rows of gherkins and his nostrils filled with the smell of mackerel. His eyes shone as he looked down at the team below. "Bingo!"

Rocky was first through the home-made window, falling softly to the concrete floor. Quickpaw sat on Dempsey's shoulders and landed quietly next to Rocky. Dempsey hauled Sunshine up and before long the Hole-in-the-Tree gang were standing in an Aladdin's cave of raccoon food. Moonlight beamed through the small hole, illuminating more goodies than a raccoon could ever imagine. Dempsey was slobbering. Rocky's tummy made funny gurgling noises.

Quickpaw Cassidy was the natural leader of the gang. He assessed the situation and whispered the orders. "Genius to get us inside Sunshine," he said. "But this is where the project really begins. If we play it right we can secure enough food for the whole winter." He grabbed a bag of birdseed. "For Headbanger," he said. "It's the least we can do. You guys fetch the food and I'll sort out a bag."

The raccoons went silently about their business. A small mountain of food was assembled below the hole in the wall. Quickpaw found some plastic bags. He leapt up to the hole and threw them into the outside world. "Now the tricky part," he whispered, explaining the system.

Dempsey waited on the outside. Quickpaw sat in the hole. Rocky and Sunshine took turns throwing tins, packets and bottles to Quickpaw. He caught them and threw them to Dempsey who was chief bagger. The raid lasted less than fifteen minutes.

Three bags would probably have been enough. But the raccoons couldn't resist going for four. They had built up a decent rhythm, and confidence had tipped into over-confidence. Rocky clasped a pot of jam and prepared to throw it to his leader when suddenly there was an almighty crash from the room next door. The guard dog barked furiously. Rocky's fur went on end as he imagined being torn to pieces by a ferocious Alsatian. The raccoons heard more crashing and banging, the dog's barks turning into whimpers of fear. Glass smashed and shelves came crashing down. The raccoons heard muffled footsteps overhead as the store owner sprinted across the landing, then light flooded under the crack in the door.

Quickpaw knew better than to hang around and investigate. Theirs was a secret raid. Whatever was going on in Max's shop was waking the whole village and, judging by the racket, it was bigger than a raccoon. There was more smashing of windowpanes as Quickpaw and Rocky leapt from the hole into the snow. They saw a flash of white as Dempsey's tail disappeared into the woods. There was no time to drag the bags of food. This was a life or death moment. They left their stolen goods and scampered towards the line of trees. They didn't need to look back; the sound of Max's shotgun said it all.

CHAPTER 2

Bear Feet

Max woke with a start. He was nimble for an old man and burglars always gave him an extra spring in his step. He thumped the light switch and leapt from his bed. He was sprinting across the landing before his wife realised what was going on. The dog was barking wildly. "What's happening?" she wailed.

"Thieving raccoons," shouted Max as a series of massive crashes and smashes were heard from the shop. Max yanked open his gun cupboard and pulled out his favourite 12-bore shotgun. He cocked it and inserted two cartridges, his hands shaking with excitement. He snapped his gun shut and made for the shop. The old man yanked open the door and the dog flew towards him, its tail between its legs. Max was surprised. Why would his dog be scared of raccoons?

He pointed the muzzle of the gun inside the shop and pulled the light cord.

Light flooded the shop, illuminating a scene of total devastation. The front door had been bashed in and his shelves pulled over. "What on earth?" muttered Max under his breath. Cold air blasted through the smashed windows and Max felt a chill under his pyjama collar. "This ain't no raccoon raid." There was glass everywhere so Max stepped his bare feet into a pair of wellington boots. He crunched around the shop, gun pointing and his trigger finger itching.

He heard a yell outside and it made him jump. He pulled the trigger and a shot rang out, blasting a hole in the ceiling. "Who's there?" he yelled, edging towards the broken window.

"It's me, Uncle Max. Don't shoot."

"What on earth was that?" puffed Rocky, huddled in the safety of a redwood tree with the rest of the Hole-in-the-Tree gang. They had an excellent view of the village and watched as the action unfurled below. They saw the village begin to light up as people were woken by the commotion. Windows opened and heads peered out. A man walked out of the forest and headed towards Max's store.

"Raymond?" shouted Max into the darkness. "Is that you, Raymond? Are you OK?"

"I think I'm OK, Uncle Max," yelled
the voice. "Did you see the bear?"

Max crunched his way to the shattered window and peered out into the snowy night. He took a flashlight and shone it out into the street. A young man came into view, his face ashen. "There was a bear, Unc," he stammered. "A big, brown grizzly. And he sure was in a bad mood."

Max stepped outside on to the veranda and his nephew limped up the steps to meet him. The men were wearing identical blue and white stripy pyjamas. "I heard a noise," explained Raymond, panting like a steam train. "And I came downstairs, Unc. Thought it might be raccoons."

Max nodded. "A menace," he agreed.

"But it weren't raccoons, Uncle Max. The door caved in and a bear threw me around the shop. I got your bat, Unc – the one you keep for burglars – and whacked him good and proper. 'Take that, you grizzly monster. You ain't stealing my Unc's food.' And I keep on hitting him, Uncle Max. But he chased me and I think he knocked some shelves over."

Max's eyes were wild. He nodded in amazement. "And he escaped through the winda, Unc, so I keep on chasin' him. Out into the snow. Looky here. Here's his big grizzly footprints."

Max's torch picked out the bear's prints. "And he headed for the trees. And that's when you showed up and I heard the gunshot and everything."

A small crowd had gathered, villagers

in pyjamas and dressing gowns; some carrying torches, some pitchforks. "Sounds like your young nephew saved your shop," panted Miriam from the cafe. "He's a hero! If he hadn't chased that old grizzly into the forest, who knows what might have happened?"

Max lowered his shotgun and hugged his nephew. "Raymond," he said. "Your ma's wrong about you. You're a good boy."

"But it's still winter," said Tyrone from the hardware store. "Grizzlies don't surface till the spring. They should be hibernating."

"W—well this one most certainly

wasn't sleeping," stammered Raymond. "My uncle's shop proves that. And the footprints in the snow. And it's nearly spring, ain't it? Maybe this old critter just woke early. Maybe it's global warmin'?"

"I guess he was just plain old hungry," nodded Max. "Hungry enough to trash my shop," he said, casting a rueful glance at the damage. "Come on, nephew, let's get you back inside. Maybe things will look better in the daylight."

The raccoons watched as the humans went back to their houses and one by one the lights went out. Sunshine persuaded the gang to go back for their supplies. "Just one bag," he said. "Otherwise our raid was for nothing."

"But what about the bear?" asked Rocky.

"Stay on red alert, boys," suggested Quickpaw. "One bag and we'll be away."

The four raccoons slunk back to Max's, remaining in the shadows at all times. Rocky was extra nervous now that a bear had been added to the hazards. They picked up the heaviest carrier bag and carried it aloft. They made their way silently across the road and followed the bear's pawprints. "He's a big fella," said Dempsey, looking at the size of the prints.

Quickpaw stopped and sniffed the air. "Waddaya smell, guys?" he asked, his nose twitching in the crisp mountain breeze.

The gang stopped, noses to the breeze. "Nothing, boss," replied Dempsey.

"And what's the one thing we know about bears?"

"That they're always in a bad mood?" piped up Dempsey. "That's why we call them grizzly."

"And the other thing?" prompted Quickpaw.

"They stink," said Rocky, pinching his nose. "Everyone knows that bears poo in the woods."

Quickpaw's nose went to one of the pawprints. He put his keen raccoon nose to the ground and sniffed again. "And nothing here either," he said, his raccoon eyebrows furrowed in puzzlement. "Very curious. This bear has no smell."

CHAPTER 3

Ivan the Terrible

The raccoons spent the night huddled together in their den, their tummies squeaking with hunger. Quickpaw knew that leadership wasn't always about being popular, and he decided the food was to be rationed. "The villagers are on alert," he explained. "So food raids are out for the time being. The lake is frozen so there's no chance of fish. We have to make this bag of food last as long as possible."

Dempsey slept fitfully, a silly raccoon grin on his face as he dreamed of apples, chutney and peanut butter. Rocky had put on his warmest pants and pulled them up to his neck. But the cold got through to his bony body and he shivered his way through the night. Quickpaw curled his bushy tail round the gang in an attempt to keep them warm. As leader he knew his job was to keep his friends safe and keep their tummies full. This was his toughest leadership test.

Quickpaw didn't sleep a wink. As Rocky's teeth chattered, his mind played out some cunning plans. But even his creative genius was struggling to come up with a plan that would see them through the winter. He looked at the carrier bag of food and thought things through. He reckoned it would last one week at most. This was going to be a very tough winter.

The sun came up and Quickpaw unfurled his tail, allowing the chill to wake Rocky and Dempsey. The raccoons stretched, yawned and shivered. Quickpaw allowed them an apple and one scoop of apricot jam each. The troop sat on the branch outside their den and surveyed the scene below.

The snow was thick and a biting wind chased through the trees. The villagers were going about their business. Max and his nephew were hammering at his windows, boarding them up to keep out the chill. The bakery was doing brisk business. Dempsey had peered in through the window once and he imagined how warm and cosy it would be right now, with the smell of fresh bread and the ovens on full blast. He wiped the slobber from his mouth. "Sure am peckish," he complained, licking the jam from his whiskers.

"We all are," said Quickpaw. "We have to be strong. We have two months of deepest winter left."

"And about a week's worth of food," continued Sunshine. "So we'd better get used to being hungry."

Rocky's shoulders wilted. He nipped back inside and put on an extra pair of pants, his favourite Superman ones.

"We need a plan," he said, returning to the branch. "Quickpaw, any ideas?"

Three pairs of beady eyes fixed on

their leader. He always had a plan. Or an idea. Quickpaw looked into the distance. "I have an idea..." he began.

Dempsey jumped for joy and nearly lost his footing. "A plan!" he whooped. "We're saved. The boss has an idea!"

"It's a high-risk strategy," continued the raccoon leader, his eyes telling Dempsey to calm down. "The village is off limits for a while," he explained. "They're on bear alert. And if a bear raided the shop and stole the food, I figure that what we need to do is find the bear."

Rocky's paw slapped across his face in despair. "That's not a strategy," he sobbed. "It's a death wish."

"If a bear raided Max's shop," Quickpaw went on, "then the bear will have some food. So we don't raid Max's store. We raid the bear's store."

Rocky paced up and down the branch. "These might be Superman pants, boss," he cried, "but I ain't no superhero. Me versus a grumbling grizzly? It's no contest."

"There are four of us," reminded Quickpaw. "And we have the forest's cleverest raccoon," he said, pointing to Sunshine. "Breaking and entering is his middle name."

"It's Darius, actually," noted Dempsey.

"There's only one grizzly in the forest," Quickpaw continued. "Ivan. And we know where his cave is."

"Ivan the Terrible?" gasped Rocky. "We're going to break into Ivan's cave and steal his food?"

"No," soothed Quickpaw Cassidy. "*Sunshine* is going to break into Ivan's cave and steal his food."

"It's impossible!" shrieked Rocky,

tugging nervously at the elastic in his pants.

Three pairs of raccoon eyes fell on Sunshine. His half-tail wilted ever so slightly, but his face remained upbeat. He raised an eyebrow and tilted the brim of his hat. He knew that breaking into a dark cave and dicing with an angry bear was going to be his most difficult mission ever. He also knew the survival of the gang depended on him making it happen. "Guys," he nodded, "there ain't no such thing as impossible."

CHAPTER 4

Rocky Rescue

The raccoons shimmied down their tree. This was most certainly a high-risk plan, but as Quickpaw had told them, Plan B was to sit in their treehouse and slowly starve to death. "Doing something is always better than doing nothing," he explained. "I learned that from Grandpa Jeffrey."

"Was that just before he got eaten by a bear?" asked Dempsey.

"Hey, guys, check out these pawprints," yelled Rocky, pointing to some huge marks in the snow. "Ivan's even bigger than I remember."

"And he's usually asleep at this time of year," Sunshine reminded them, "so he's likely to be even more grizzly than normal."

The raccoons followed the bear prints for a few hundred yards before the trail abruptly stopped. Three raccoon noses hit the ground, sniffing for clues. Quickpaw stood tall like a meerkat, eyes peeled.

"That big old grizzly just stopped, right here," said Dempsey. "But there's no tracks and no smell or nothing. How can a 500-kilo bear just disappear?"

"Here are some more prints," yelled Rocky. "But they're wellington boots.

A person! And by the looks of them they headed back to the village."

"You don't think Ivan ate a person?" gulped Dempsey. "That's very bad."

Quickpaw scratched his head. This was turning into a real crime scene. He knew Ivan's cave was just ahead so he beckoned the gang forward. They hopped through a deep snowdrift and stood at the entrance of Ivan's cave. The raccoons were even more puzzled when they heard deep snores echoing from within. Ivan was clearly deep in hibernation.

"There's no way that big bad guy has been awake recently," said Sunshine. "That's one very deeeep sleeeep." He bravely wandered into the cave and gave the sleeping bear a prod just to prove his point. The other raccoons saw a flash of light as Sunshine took a snap of the sleeping bear.

He sauntered out of the cave and showed the picture to the gang. "So if Ivan didn't break into Max's shop, who did?" thought Quickpaw aloud.

"Another bear might have moved into our forest?" suggested Sunshine.

Before they had time to think this through a shot rang out and a bullet sent up a shower of snow. The raccoons looked to Quickpaw, who led by example, darting to a nearby tree.

"Something moved!" yelled a voice. "Might be that savage old grizzly."

"Yikes," squeaked Rocky. "There's a posse after the bear. They're going to kill Ivan. And it wasn't even him who did it.

He was asleep! He still is!"

"We have to protect Ivan," said Dempsey. "It's so unfair."

Sunshine was ahead of the game. He left his hat and camera behind as he shimmied up a tree. The others watched him leaping from branch to branch, sending snow showers on to the villagers below. Guns pointed skyward and shots resounded through the forest. Flocks of birds erupted from the trees, squawking in terror. There was confusion below and the villagers turned and followed the snowfalls, convinced they were on the trail of a grizzly. More shots exploded upwards, pellets blasting away the leaves to Sunshine's left.

The exhausted Sunshine led the villagers away from Ivan's cave. An almighty blast took away the branch he was on and he fell through the trees, landing in a heap in the snow. He climbed out of a raccoon-shaped hole and found himself circled by angry villagers.

"It's not a bear," exclaimed a man, pointing a shotgun at Sunshine's face.

Sunshine felt himself all over. *Correct*, he thought. *It's a lovely, cuddly, friendly raccoon.*

"Let's do him anyway," yelled an angry voice. "We want blood."

Sunshine put his paws across his face

and awaited his fate. Rocky swung from tree to tree on the trail of his friend. He looked down at Sunshine and saw the barrel of a gun pointing at the terrified raccoon. He didn't know what to do. All he knew was that he had to do something. Quickpaw's words echoed in his head... *Doing something is always better than doing nothing.*

He jumped from the tree and landed beside his friend. The raccoon stood tall, hands on hips. The villagers looked shocked. The raccoon's Superman pants were pulled up high and proud.

McCluskey beckoned to the villagers to lower their guns. "It's one of them critters,"

he said. "I recognise the pants. This one helped save Max's life. Remember last season when robbers broke in?"

There was a murmuring of agreement. "Let these guys go. We owe them. It's that bad old bear that we're after. Breaking into Max's shop. And then causing the flood." One or two of the men looked disappointed as they trudged off into the snow.

Rocky and Sunshine collapsed into the snow in relief. They were hauled to their feet by Dempsey and Quickpaw. Sunshine's hat was plonked on his head and Rocky was held aloft like the hero he was. Quickpaw motioned that now was the right time to investigate the flood, and they all followed, approaching the village with caution. The scene that met their eyes was more awful than they could ever have imagined.

CHAPTER 5

Dam Buster

The torrent had gushed through the centre of the village and the muddy water had washed away at least three houses. A path of sludge blighted the main road. Residents slipped and slid their way through the mud, some hosing their doorsteps, others sweeping debris away. Several cars were turned over. The snowy white scene of earlier had been replaced by a sludgy brown mess.

Max was boarding up his windows after last night's bear attack. His neighbour was banging a 'for sale' sign into the gloop. "I've had enough," he complained to Max. "Look at the mess! We're finished." The bottom of his wife's nightdress was trailing in mud and she sloshed through the mire, angrily sweeping slush from the doorstep.

"Last summer it was raccoons. That was bad enough. This season it's bears."

"It's a terrible shame," agreed Raymond.

"But I reckon you're right – it's time to move on. That grizzly's downright dangerous. I saw him up at the dam. It'll live with me forever. That old bear crashing through the dam, causing this awful flood. Biggest grizzly I ever did see. I'm amazed nobody's died." Max's nephew took a poster and nailed it to Max's shop. He stood back to examine his handiwork. He'd Googled a picture of an angry-looking grizzly bear and pasted it on to a page of A4. 'Wanted' read the simple caption, 'Dead'.

"I'm surprised you're not selling up, Uncle Max," said Raymond. "Everyone else seems to be."

The old man looked at the scene of

devastation. The hardware store and pizza parlour already had 'For Sale' signs up. He knew others would follow.

"I've lived here all my life," said Max, a tear rolling down his weathered cheek. "And I ain't gonna let a critter scare me away."

"But property prices are falling, Unc. Your shop will soon be worthless." He pointed up the muddy street where McCluskey had just started putting up a 'For Sale' sign outside his house. "You'll be living in a ghost town."

"That's as may be," grunted Max, hammering a nail into his windowframe. "But it'll take something extra special to get me moving, Raymond."

The raccoons watched from their favourite tree. They saw a picture of a bear being hammered to Max's porch. "First a bear. And now a flood," mused Quickpaw. "That's a lifetime of bad luck in one day! Come on, guys, let's investigate."

He led the Hole-in-the-Tree gang down the tree and they scampered through the snow, following the river upstream towards the top of the village. Dempsey gasped at the scene. A huge hole had been bashed through the dam and the river was pouring through. "That was one of our favourite fishing spots," whimpered Rocky. "Ruined. By a bear."

Sunshine shook his head. "But how could it be by a bear? Ivan is fast asleep," he reminded them. "Something's not right."

The gang crept closer to the dam. A beaver surfaced and Quickpaw beckoned to him. Beavers and raccoons had enjoyed an uneasy peace since the Canadian Fish Wars of 2005. They shared similar diets and language. "Over here," shouted Quickpaw. The beaver flipped his tail and glided over to the bank.

"Dishashter," mumbled the beaver through his huge teeth. "Water levelsh dropped by ten feet. It's up to us guysh to fixsh it."

"Timmmberrr!" yelled a beaver from the other side of the lake. The raccoons watched as a pine tree twisted and fell, crashing into the water. Several beavers set to work, gnawing branches into made-to-measure lengths that would fill the gap perfectly.

"What happened?" asked Quickpaw.

"Not shure, buddy," admitted the beaver. "Humansh made the dam. Very well built as a matter of fact. And our preliminary inveshtigashons point to humansh destroying it."

"Not bears?" asked Dempsey.

The beaver dissolved into fits of laughter. "Beverley's down there looking

at the damage ash we speak," he wheezed.
"Besht darn engineer in the beaver
brigade. And I'll fall off a log if she comes
up with 'bear damage' in her report."

"Can we take a look at the dam?" asked
Rocky.

The beaver stopped laughing and

eyed the raccoons suspiciously. His face twitched and he picked at his huge front teeth. "You guysh done your health and shafety?" The raccoons looked at each other and shrugged. "You need level three," continued the beaver. "Tree felling is level one," he explained, waving a paw at the newly felled tree. "Bashic level beaver shtuff. Chomping logs and floating them on to the river is level two. But fitting logs into a dam and anything underwater is level three. High rishk, you shee. I'd need to see your shertificatsh."

"We've got raccoon level four," argued quick-thinking Sunshine. "Tree climbing. Can you beavers climb trees?"

The argument was just heating up as Beverly surfaced, sucking in a lungful of fresh mountain air. She glided over to the foreman to give her report.

"What did you find, engineer?" asked the foreman. "These boys are intereshted in bearsh. Is this grishly damage?"

Beverly the beaver spat out a mouthful of water. "Might be," she said, "if bears know enough about electronicsh and exploshions." Beverly held out her paw to reveal a  small remote control. "My investigashions show the dam was holed by a shmall exploshion, triggered remotely by thish device. Whoever blew it threw the detonator into the water before they left. Bears? Nope.

Shomebody blew a hole in the dam."
Beverly watched the beady raccoon
eyes grow large at the news. "And that
shomebody had to be a human."

CHAPTER 6

The 'Accident'

The raccoons returned to their den and sat on their branch, dangling their feet. Quickpaw and Sunshine were quiet, lost in thought. To their right the villagers were buzzing around, some cleaning mud from their doorsteps and others hammering 'For Sale' signs outside their homes and shops. The raccoons were in a glum mood. "If Max closes, we're doomed," panicked Rocky. "He's our food store. Our lifeline."

To their left was the icy lake. "Guys, check this out," said Dempsey, pointing to a man pulling a canoe towards the shore. The raccoons watched as the man pushed the boat into the water and leapt aboard. He hit the thin ice with the paddle and the boat slid effortlessly towards the middle of the lake. Sunshine went inside and returned with some binoculars that he'd stolen from a tourist.

"See if these give you a better view," he

said, handing them to Dempsey.

"Nope," said his friend. "The man's got smaller. Can hardly see him at all."

Sunshine grabbed the binoculars and turned them the right way round. "Now try," he said.

"Wowza," began Dempsey, nearly falling off the branch with shock. "He's right there in front of me!" he said, reaching his paw out to see if he could touch the man. "These sure are magical goggles."

"What can you see?" hissed Sunshine, reaching for his camera and zooming in.

"It's Max's nephew," said Dempsey.

"Guess he's going fishing. Except there's no rod."

The other raccoons strained to see. "He's taking his shoes off," said Dempsey, "and the boat sure is rocking."

Quickpaw nodded. "And what's he doing now?" asked his friend impatiently. "Looks like he's shaping to dive in."

Sunshine clicked his camera, capturing Raymond mid-dive. There was a silent splash from the lake. "He has!" commentated Dempsey. "He must be mad. The water's freezing. He's gone and jumped right in through the broken ice."

Quickpaw snatched the binoculars to see for himself. The raccoons could hear

Raymond screaming. Quickpaw was getting a close-up of the action. Raymond was splashing around frantically, yelling at the top of his voice. Quickpaw's binoculars cut to the village. Max had heard the yells and was running towards the lake. He shouted to others and soon there was a small gang of villagers at the lakeside.

"Help! Quickly," yelled Raymond, splashing and spluttering in the middle of the lake. "It's cold. It was a bear."

Two burly men jumped into a rowing boat and cut their way through the ice. They reached the drowning man and hauled him aboard. The Hole-in-the-Tree gang watched as the boat came to shore and the freezing man was hurried back to the village. Quickpaw saw Raymond pointing to the 'Wanted' poster as he was huddled in a blanket and helped indoors.

The raccoons looked at each other in total puzzlement. "He seemed to be blaming the bear," suggested Quickpaw. "Again."

"And we know that there was no bear," said Dempsey. "I mean, he just plain jumped into that freezing water. We saw it with our own raccoon eyes."

"I don't get it," said Rocky. "First Max's place is trashed and there are bear tracks but no smell."

"Then the dam bursts and Max's nephew reckons it's a bear. But it's a bomb," piped up Sunshine.

"And now Raymond jumps into the lake and blames a non-existent grizzly," continued Sunshine. "Two themes run through everything: bears and Raymond."

"And," said Quickpaw, "we know that Ivan is fast asleep. He's not the problem. So I suggest we investigate Raymond." He cracked his raccoon knuckles and eyed his friends before nodding to Sunshine. "I think it's time for another secret raid."

CHAPTER 7

Still Life

The snow fell silently. The Hole-in-the-Tree gang waited on the warmest roof in the village: the bakery. It'd been an hour since Raymond's bedroom light had gone out so they figured the man must be asleep.

"Clues," whispered the raccoon leader. "Something's not right. We can't have Max selling up and moving away or we're doomed. So let's see what we can find. This is a mystery and it needs solving."

Sunshine led the way. The light-fingered raccoon put his claws under the window frame and pulled. Nothing happened, so he beckoned to his friends and they all stood in a line and inserted their claws under the frame, like weightlifters waiting for their moment. "After three," hissed Sunshine. "One, two, and... three!"

The Hole-in-the-Tree gang heaved as a team and the window creaked upwards, just enough for four skinny critters to scramble through. They fell silently through the curtains on to the carpeted floor. They were on the first-floor landing. A dim light lit the scene and Quickpaw put his paw up to stifle Rocky's gasp. The whites of his terrified eyes shone as he pointed all around. "Dead animals!" he muffled from behind Quickpaw's fingers. "What did I tell you?"

Max's landing was decorated with an array of stuffed animals: crows, eagles, ferrets, even a beaver, its fake white teeth glinting in the moonlight. A moose's head stuck out from the wall.

"Seems Max doesn't just hunt for fun," whispered Quickpaw, letting go of Rocky.

"Looks like he stuffs the animals. Why would anyone do that?"

"Maybe he eats them?" whimpered Rocky, his teeth chattering once more.

"Then we need to be even more careful," advised Sunshine.

The raccoons crept along the landing, sniffing under each door. "Max and Mrs Max," said Dempsey. "I can smell his breath."

The next door was slightly open. Quickpaw peeked in. He could hear gentle breathing from the bed. "This is Raymond's room," he whispered.

"Quietly," warned Sunshine, staring at Dempsey and clasping his paw over

Rocky's chattering teeth.

"S-s-s-sorry," sniffed Rocky. "It's just that Max has a baseball bat, a gun and a dog. And he stuffs dead animals and puts them on a shelf!"

Quickpaw put his paw to his ear and the raccoons listened to Raymond's gentle snoring. "Humans are dangerous," he reminded them. "So it's in, search and out." The raccoons tiptoed to the four corners of the bedroom. Quickpaw found the linen basket, filled with wet clothes and smelly pants. *Not good!*

Sunshine started under the bed, rummaging in the dust. *Nothing.* He jumped on to a chest of drawers, carefully opening each one and examining the contents. *More nothing!*

Rocky rummaged through a few clothes and some boots, sniffing furiously. He wasn't sure what he was looking for, but fear had been replaced by excitement. It was great to be part of the team. He swung on the wardrobe door and it creaked open. The raccoons fell silent as Raymond stirred. His hand flopped down the side of the bed, right in front of Dempsey's face. His hand stroked the raccoon. "Tiddles," he croaked. "My favourite pussy cat." Raymond stroked the startled raccoon a couple of times before his breathing deepened and he was in slumber once more. Dempsey carefully prised himself out of Raymond's grasp and joined Quickpaw in the wardrobe.

"Here," hissed Dempsey. "Look at these." He held up a huge slipper. "There's two of them."

"Biggest shoes I've ever seen!" gasped Quickpaw. Sunshine found a torch and clicked it on. He shone it upwards and picked out his friends in the wardrobe. They held up the slippers.

"Giant feet," squealed Rocky. "As big as a bear's! And look at the shape. Same as a bear's."

"I reckon Raymond here's been sneaking around the woods in bear feet."

"Bare feet?" tutted Dempsey. "That'd be really cold."

"No! Not 'bare' as in 'naked'. *Bear* feet. Feet like *bears*!" explained Quickpaw, holding the giant shoes aloft. Just then the torch dazzled Dempsey and he scrabbled at the wardrobe before falling to the ground with a thud and a startled squeal.

Raymond woke with a start. "What? Who?" he began, his hand scrabbling for the light switch. Rocky was already halfway out of the window. His pants got caught, but he was freed by Quickpaw. Dempsey was winded. He rolled under the bed and winced in pain as the light came on. He watched as Raymond's feet hit the floor and he heard the man yell as he picked up a giant bear slipper and waved it at the escaping raccoons.

Sunshine was the coolest raccoon in the forest. He stood on the windowsill and reached under his hat. There was a blinding flash as he captured Raymond waving a giant bear foot at him and then the half-tailed raccoon was away into the night. For a second Raymond imagined he must be dreaming. The camera flash temporarily blinded him and he staggered towards the half-opened window. Dempsey took his chance and sneaked on to the landing.

Max's nephew opened the window fully and peered out into the night. The man rubbed his eyes in disbelief as he spotted three raccoons shimmying down the drainpipe. He could have sworn that one of them was wearing Superman Y-fronts.

He pulled on a dressing gown and went out on to the landing.

Max had heard the kerfuffle and met him on the landing. "What is it, Raymond?" he croaked. "Dreaming about bears?"

"Raccoons, Unc," he said. "I think there were some in my room."

Max looked angry. He remembered how the Hole-in-the-Tree gang used to break into his store. And how one day last year they'd come to his rescue and saved his life. "I thought we had a truce," he snarled. "If I catch 'em, they'll end up like these critters." Max swept his arm across the landing where hundreds of stuffed animals sat in suspended animation. Max was an expert hunter and this was his lifetime's work. Raymond picked up a buzzard and marvelled at its lifelike qualities. Its feathers were dry and its eyes glassy, but it was a splendid piece of work.

Dempsey's escape plan had stalled when Max appeared on the landing. He looked around at the stuffed animals and decided it was his best chance. *My only chance! Stand still and look stuffed!* The raccoon gulped as Raymond walked past him. Dempsey sat as still as he could, in what he considered to be his cute pose. *Please don't look too closely*, he thought. Max stopped and peered at the raccoon.

Don't blink. Don't blink. Or sneeze! Or breathe!

"They sure are lifelike, Unc," he purred as he picked up the stuffed red squirrel next to Dempsey. Raymond took a close look at the squirrel. "Genius," he whispered to himself. "Just like the real thing." He placed the squirrel back on the table.

Dempsey wanted to blink so badly it hurt. Raymond stared right into his petrified raccoon eyes. "Amazing," he grinned, breathing pickled-onion breath into Dempsey's face. Nothing moved except Dempsey's eyelids. It was the quickest blink he'd ever done. Raymond wasn't the brightest. It was fortunate for Dempsey that it was 3am and Raymond's brain was even dimmer than usual.

"It's a hobby," said Max. "Shoot 'em. Stuff 'em. Look at 'em. If I see any more raccoons, or bears, for that matter, they'll end up stuffed. In fact," he thought aloud,

"I'm looking for a raccoon. It's the one critter that's missing from my collection."

It took Raymond a second or two to register. He looked at his uncle and scratched his head. "A raccoon, Uncle Max? But you've got one." He turned back to the table. "Right he—" he began, pointing to an empty spot on the table. Raymond blinked hard. The squirrel and buzzard were still there. He scanned the table, his mouth gaping open like the trout on the shelf above.

Dempsey huddled under the table, adrenaline coursing through his body. He was catching up with some blinking and his chest was heaving. The terrified raccoon was desperate to run, but his small raccoon brain was controlling the urge. He heard the men talking. He watched the men's feet slope back to the other ends of the landing and breathed a sigh of relief as they disappeared back to their bedrooms. The first rays of sun were glowing over the horizon as Dempsey crept quietly downstairs and escaped through the bathroom window.

He made his way through the sludge and snow. He sat and watched as three lorries trundled into the village. Little did the raccoons know that today their sleepy little home was to become headline news.

CHAPTER 8

The Meeting

The raccoons spent most of the next day watching events unfold in the village. They'd never seen it so busy. Several television camera crews had set up in the high street. Every hotel room was booked and the village was flooded with muddy strangers. There were television crews at the lake where Raymond had fallen in. Some visited the burst dam. Most flocked around the village, talking to the residents – most of whom were shaking their heads.

Max's nephew seemed to be at the centre of everything. Quickpaw and Sunshine sat outside the electrical store and watched an interview on a flat-screen television. "It started with a raid on my uncle's shop," said a grave-looking Raymond. "The biggest grizzly I ever did see," he said, raising his arms and bearing his teeth for dramatic effect. The camera zoomed in on the 'Wanted' poster nailed to Max's shop.

"The residents say you were a hero that night," prompted the reporter.

"I did what any citizen would have done," said Raymond, trying to look bashful. "I chased the critter off."

"But the killer bear returned," probed the reporter, putting on her serious face.

"Broke the dam," wailed Raymond, his finger pointing towards the top of the village. "We were flooded. The village is devastated."

The cameraman turned and took a wide-angle view of the muddy street. He zoomed in on the fishing tackle store, where the owner was hammering

a 'sold' sign into the ground. Then the picture turned back to Raymond. "And tell us what happened with your boating accident."

"It was no accident, lady," said

Raymond, tears filling his eyes. "I went
fishing, minding my own business, when
the grizzly took my boat out. Bang, crash.
And there I am, viewers, fighting for my
life in a frozen lake. I'm thankful to these

good people for saving my bacon. That bear's gonna kill someone soon, I tells ya," he said, emotion rising in his voice. "Don't mind so much if it's me, but I don't want it to be a little child," he wailed, overdoing the drama.

The camera cut back to the reporter. "A dramatic eye-witness account for *Eye-Witness News*," she said cheesily. "It's no wonder that over half the villagers have put their properties up for sale." She finished proudly with a line she'd been trying to squeeze in since the day began. "If you go down to the woods in this neighbourhood, you are most definitely in for a big surprise!

Back to Clint and Natasha in the studio."

Quickpaw figured that morale needed boosting, so the raccoons spent the rest of the day comfort-eating. Rocky was chattering nonstop about anything doom and gloom. They finished off their entire bag of goodies and sat with their tummies full but heads empty of ideas. As the sun set on another day they watched as the television crews packed up and made their way to the next bad-news town.

"We're doomed," moaned Rocky. "Raymond's bear story has ruined our village."

The raccoons huddled together in their den and slept. Except Quickpaw. His keen brain was buzzing. The villagers seemed to be sleepwalking into selling up and leaving. And from what Quickpaw could make out, it was all to do with Raymond's imaginary bear. He left his sleeping partners and made his way through the crisp forest snow to the muddy sludge of the village.

It was unusually quiet, except for the village hall. Quickpaw sat on the windowsill and peered in. It was a full house. Every villager was there. The raccoon couldn't work out what was going on, but at the end it seemed like a deal had been done.

A man in a suit was shaking a lot of hands. Quickpaw noticed that Max did no handshaking and his face was like thunder. He couldn't miss the grin on Raymond's face. "Like a raccoon with a fresh river salmon," muttered Quickpaw under his breath.

While the villagers were busy it seemed a good idea to take advantage of the situation. Quickpaw knew the gang needed food and PizzaHouse was their favourite place to forage. He slunk round the back and peered into the skip. He grabbed a bag and filled it with some thrown-away crusts. He sauntered to the front where he knew the bin always contained the best pickings.

He was busy rummaging when a huge four-by-four truck pulled up and Raymond jumped out. Quickpaw sank into the bin, his beady eyes peering out and his nose twitching. Two minutes later Raymond reappeared carrying six extra-large pizzas. He placed them carefully on the back seat and the engine roared. *Where on earth's he going with six pizzas? At this time of night?* wondered the raccoon.

He watched the red lights of the truck disappear up the road. *He's turned right!* thought Quickpaw. *That's a single track road to the top of the mountain. Who's he meeting at the cabin? In the dead of night? With pizza?*

Quickpaw wasn't sure what was going on, but he was certain it was worth investigating. *We need to be in that truck,* he thought as he sprinted across the forest towards his gang.

CHAPTER 9

Hitching a Ride

Quickpaw was shouting for his friends to wake up as he shimmied up the redwood tree. Sunshine was already wide awake. Dempsey was just coming round and Rocky was stepping into his pants as the raccoon leader burst into the den.

"Emergency, guys," he panted. "Raymond's up to something. Not sure what's going on, but my raccoon instincts tell me the villagers are in major trouble. Whatever Max's nephew's up to, I'm betting it's bad news."

The raccoons arrived at the bend in the road just in time. Raymond's truck had weaved its way through the forest on the steady incline up the mountain. It was dark and snowy so he was driving extra carefully. The Hole-in-the-Tree gang had gone direct, straight as an arrow, heading for the overhanging tree on the slow bend. They hung on as the truck roared into sight, its powerful headlights dazzling the raccoons.

"When I say now…" ordered Quickpaw. "We only get one chance at this."

The truck slowed as it approached the

tight bend. "Now!" squeaked the leader, and four sets of claws let go. They fell silently into the back of the four-by-four, furry stowaways on an uphill adventure.

The truck wound its way up the steep mountainside. Rocky gave up watching, the sheer drop making his tummy feel funny. After a while, the truck pulled into a snowy clearing. Light flooded from the log cabin's windows. Raymond parked his truck next to three others. The raccoons heard the car door open and they smelled freshly cooked pizza as he strode to the cabin. The cabin door opened and slammed shut. Dempsey's nose twitched out from under the plastic cover. His eyes followed.

"It's beautiful," he gasped. "I've never been so high up!" Above them a perfectly clear night sky, the full moon as bright as a torch. Below them the village lights were equally beautiful, twinkling in the valley.

Quickpaw led the way, skipping out of the back of the truck into the deep snow. Rocky landed in a deep drift and had to be hauled out by his pants. The raccoons struggled through the snow towards a window. They peeped in. There were a dozen men in the cabin, looking, to the raccoons, like characters in a silent movie. They seemed very happy and Raymond was being slapped on the back. He was presented with a bottle of beer. The pizzas were opened and the men pulled away big slices, scoffing hungrily.

Dempsey's tummy broke the silence. "I'm imagining the smell. And the taste," he said, his eyes rolling and his tongue drooling. "Hawaiian!" he said, swaying his arms in a hula-hula dance. "My absolute favouritest."

Sunshine was working on a plan to get them inside. While the others focused on the food, he was scanning for entry points. It was freezing at the top of the mountain, so all windows and doors had been sealed. He spotted a fireplace. He knew from experience that fireplaces had chimneys. If the gang wanted some pizza and, more importantly, to solve the mystery, then that was their only entry point.

Three drooling raccoons followed the Sunshine Cub up the drainpipe on to the slippery roof. They scrabbled to the ridge, dislodging small avalanches of snow on the way. Sunshine's face peered into the chimney and he took in a huge whiff of warm pizza. He knew this was the only way he would ever convince his friends to enter the danger zone, so he encouraged them to share the smell. Dempsey's tummy did his thinking for him and Sunshine had to stop him clambering straight down the chimney.

"We have to be silent," warned Sunshine. "It's our only way in. And our only way out. The men are sitting at the table at the moment so this is a good time to arrive. They're distracted by food."

Dempsey wasn't listening. His nose was sniffing and he had his ga-ga eyes on. "Fooood…"

"So the plan is that we lower ourselves

towards the fireplace and hang upside down so we can see what's going on."

"Like bats?" asked Rocky.

"Exactly like bats," agreed Sunshine. "Bats with a picture maker," he said, patting the camera. "And when the moment is right we can listen in and maybe grab a slice of the action."

"A slice of the pizza," drooled Dempsey. "That's what I want."

Sunshine left his hat on the chimney stack. His camera was wound round his wrist. The chimney was narrow and sooty. They hoped the men wouldn't notice black snow falling in the fireplace and that they wouldn't hear Rocky's double sneeze as soot went up his delicate nostrils. The tunnel widened out at the bottom and the raccoons hung upside down in the fireplace, their feet lodged in gaps in the bricks. Four sets of ears, eyes and twitching noses peered into the cabin, observing an upside-down scene. The raccoons couldn't understand what was being said, but Sunshine kept clicking his camera.

The table was cleared and a laptop and projector set up. A huge image was beamed on to a white cabin wall. "Our village!" squeaked Rocky.

"Raymond's done a fine job," began one of the men. "Played his part to perfection.

The villagers are totally convinced that there's a dangerous bear on the loose."

The raccoons noticed that everyone was looking at Max's nephew. And he looked very pleased indeed. He held up his huge bear-pawprint shoes and everyone broke into peals of laughter.

Sunshine's camera clicked.

"They sure did fall for it," growled Raymond, stomping around the cabin in his giant feet, his fingers clawing the air, grizzly bear-style.

Click click.

"The burst dam was genius," said another of the men. "I'm glad my little explosion helped."

"And I didn't even plan the lake attack," grinned Raymond. "I just thought it up on the spur of the moment and went for it."

"It brought the news crews," purred the ringleader. "Did you see how quickly those 'For Sale' signs went up? We've convinced them that they need to sell up now, before property prices fall even further. It's a ghost town in the making."

"Which is why they went for our rescue package at the village hall last night. Our deal is a no-brainer. Sign now and take our very generous offer. Or wait until your property is worthless."

"And they all signed up last night,

right?" asked a burly man.

"All except one," grunted the man in the suit. "Raymond's stubborn uncle. That stupid old man is risking the entire project."

"Under control," grinned Raymond. "Uncle Max said it'd take something extraordinary to shift him. So I've saved the best till last."

"Remind us what the endgame is again," asked a fat man chewing on a discarded pizza crust. A laptop key was pressed and the village picture disappeared. Instead there was a gleaming hotel and spa, with log cabins dotted around the village.

Click. Sunshine nearly dropped his

camera. He was impressed.

"This is the image we've sold to the villagers," explained a man. "Told them we're property developers and that we're building a world-class eco-friendly tourist village. What did you say, Marv? 'In tune with nature?' Something equally sickly, anyway."

The laptop clicked again and the eco-village disappeared. A heavy industrial scene lit up the wall. Sunshine's camera zoomed in for a close-up. *Click click.* Chimneys, a maze of pipes and a huge factory sat in the forest clearing. An ugly road cut a scar through the woodland. Their fishing lake had disappeared.

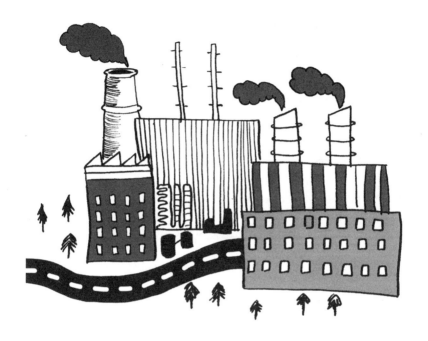

"It's dirty work," grinned the leader. "But someone's got to do it. The *real* plan is to buy up the village at knockdown prices and drill for oil. Our geologist here reckons there's millions of barrels buried deep beneath the village."

The geologist nodded. "And the only way to get at it is to remove the village and bring in the heavy gear. And we'll need to build a refinery. Not exactly eco-friendly," he coughed. "But hey, it's only a few villagers, a lake, a few trees..."

"And a killer bear," laughed Raymond.

"As for 'eco-friendly'," chuckled a man in a checked shirt, "our project isn't exactly 'green'. More... 'black'. Black gold! Raise your glasses, gentlemen, to environmental devastation and a lifetime of wealth for us all!"

CHAPTER 10

Make-up, Fake-up

The men had retreated to bed and the raccoons to the back of the four-by-four.

"Didn't much like that picture of our forest," groaned Rocky. "All that industry and all those pipes. It's not just us that'd be doomed, but every animal for miles around. Including the fish in the lake."

"My bet is that Max and the villagers have never seen that picture," said Quickpaw. "Let's stay here till morning and see what Raymond's going to do. We have evidence in this picture maker," he said, tapping his camera proudly.

The raccoons awoke at first light. Another four-by-four pulled into the clearing and a woman with a suitcase went into the cabin. "You guys stay here," ordered Quickpaw. "Sunshine and I will visit the chimney and check out the latest."

Quickpaw and Sunshine resumed their bat-like positions. The woman had opened her case and laid out brushes and paints on the table. Raymond was lying on the sofa in his boxer shorts.

"Are you any good?" he asked.

"Hollywood good, honey," said the lady. "I've worked on some of the best horror movies." Sunshine pressed the shutter button to capture the moment. "You asked for the best make-up artist in the world. Well, you've got her! Now, what is it we're after exactly?"

"Bear attack," grunted Raymond. "It needs to look convincing. I thought a huge scratch down my side, here," he said, clawing from his chest to his tummy. "And maybe a blow to the face?"

"Lovely," smiled the lady, setting to work. "And how about a bite wound on your neck for good measure."

By the time the rest of the men surfaced, Raymond was covered in gore. The bite marks on his neck were particularly convincing, deep and red and bloody.

"And check these beauties," he marvelled, lifting his ripped shirt to reveal fake grizzly bear scratches on his side.

"Impressive," said one of the men, passing a huge wad of cash to the lady. She tucked the money into her pocket and packed her case. She handed over a jar.

"When you deposit him in the forest, splash some of this around. Fake blood. It'll make the scene look even more convincing. A bear attack would leave oodles of the red stuff."

The lady left, her job done. The men discussed the rest of their plan. "Now all we have to do is get back down the mountain and for Raymond here to convince his Uncle to sell up. A savage, near-death bear attack should convince the old man that we mean *serious* business. We should have Max's Store snapped up at a knockdown price by mid-morning."

Just then, Sunshine accidentally pressed the flash button on the camera, and it made a loud, whirring sound. *Shush*, he thought as he frantically looked for the source of the noise. He fumbled with the off switch and dropped the camera. It thudded into the hearth, sending up a small cloud of ash. Worst still, it continued to beep.

One of the men walked towards the fireplace and the raccoon spies disappeared from view, hanging in the darkness. They could smell the man. The beeping seemed magnified up the chimney. They held their breath as a hand reached into the fireplace and the man removed the camera. "What's this?" he asked, dusting soot off it. "Anyone dropped their camera?"

Nobody answered the man. The raccoon faces reappeared, noses twitching nervously. They were hoping the man wouldn't look at the footage. He sauntered into the kitchen and they saw him place the camera into a drawer. Moments later the men stood and left the cabin. One of the men locked the kitchen door on the way out. The front door was slammed and locked and the upside-down raccoons heard the engines roar into life and the vehicles crunch their way through the snow.

Sunshine was frantic. All the evidence he'd carefully collected was sitting in a drawer in a locked kitchen. He and Quickpaw dropped into the fireplace and dusted themselves off.

"It's not your fault, Sunshine," said the raccoon leader. "It was beeping. You had to let go or it would have given us away." Sunshine leapt at the door handle and hung on. He rattled it, but the door was well and truly locked.

Dempsey and Rocky were hiding in

a tree. They saw their friends climbing out of the chimney pot and ran to meet them. "It's terrible," cried Rocky. "Poor Raymond has been half eaten. He's bleeding all over."

Quickpaw explained what they'd seen.

"So Raymond is faking it again?" asked Rocky.

"Yes, and we have proof. We need to get our picture-maker to Max before those men get to him first. But we have a problem... the picture-maker is in the kitchen."

"And I bet the kitchen is locked," guessed Dempsey.

"I don't like to lose," yelled Sunshine

as he watched the four-by-fours winding their way down the mountain. "There are lots of different sorts of raids. And sometimes smash-and-grab is the best way forward." He beckoned his friends to a fallen branch and together they heaved it out of the snow and struggled towards the log cabin. The raccoons made it as far as the kitchen window.

"After three," ordered Sunshine, beginning to get into a swinging rhythm. The raccoons let go and the branch sailed through the air. It hit the glass and smashed its way through. Instantly, Sunshine was on the windowsill, treading carefully. The gang watched as his back legs disappeared and his grinning face reappeared, camera in paw. "Say cheese," he smiled as the flash blinded his friends.

The gang bounded to the tyre tracks and gazed down the mountain. The four trucks were halfway down.

"We'll never get there in time," whinged Rocky. "We're stuck at the top of the mountain. We've got no transport."

"Think again, young Rocky-my-lad," yelled Sunshine, disappearing back into the kitchen. He returned thirty seconds later with a shiny tea tray. "Hang on to your pants. This is going to get exciting."

CHAPTER 11

Tea-Tray Slalom

Rocky wasn't sure.

"Come on, Rocky," Dempsey said. "The baddies are getting away. Let's do it!"

Quickpaw picked up the tray and headed to the top of the slope. "There are a lot of trees between us and the village," he noticed. "So we'll have to huddle together and lean left and right."

"And some serious bumps," noted Rocky, pacing up and down, tugging nervously at his elastic. "It's raccoon suicide."

"Or the greatest adventure in raccoon history!" yelled Dempsey.

Quickpaw calculated the odds of sledging down the mountain and arriving in one piece. The chances were slim, but so were the odds of survival in an industrial wasteland. It could be a short sharp ending with a small chance of success. Or a long, lingering, poisonous, certain death.

He jumped aboard the silver tea tray and manoeuvred into position. Dempsey jumped on too, hugging his leader tight. Sunshine was third up, wrapping his paws round Dempsey. The tray balanced at the top of the snowy slope. Three raccoon faces turned to Rocky. "We're not a gang," urged Sunshine. "We're a team of four buddies. But we can't wait forever. Max and the villagers are depending on us."

Rocky's teeth were at it again. "B-b-but—"

As Quickpaw nudged the tray towards the hill, Sunshine grabbed Rocky's knicker elastic and the reluctant raccoon was aboard, one paw hanging on to Sunshine, another covering his eyes.

"Geronimooooo!"

There wasn't much time to get used to it. Sunshine secured his cowboy hat hard down over his ears. The tray took off at full speed, skimming across the freshly sprinkled snow. The bob-sledding raccoons ducked under a low hanging branch and leant left to avoid a rock. "And right," bellowed Quickpaw, swaying his body to show the way.

"Treeee!" barked Dempsey. "Dead ahead!" Four raccoon bodies leant hard right and the tray swerved, almost losing Rocky off the back.

The animals skimmed along, the fingers of their back paws clinging to the tea-tray, their front paws locked in a terrified embrace. Quickpaw's whiskers were blowing in the wind as they approached an extra-fast straight bit. "Wooo hooo!"

Just as they thought they were getting the hang of it the tray hit a bump and the raccoons took off. They sailed through the air and landed with a thump. Sunshine held on to Rocky's pants and hauled him back on board. "There are the cars," called Dempsey, daring to release a paw and pointing at the convoy of vehicles meandering their way down the mountain. "We're gaining!"

It was perfect downhill conditions and

the tray was
moving at an
incredible pace.
Four pairs of ears were
flat against raccoon heads
and their eyes squinted into the
chilly mountain air. The team leant left.
Then right and another right to avoid a
fir tree.

Quickpaw's whiskers were frosting up. "Another jump!" warned the leader as the tray took off again. This was a high one. The tray leapt silently into the air. Paws gripped the side of the sledge as they jumped across the road in front of the first jeep.

The driver slid to a stop as the tray flew across the road. He turned to Raymond. "Did you see that?" he asked, his eyes wide in amazement.

Raymond did a double blink and his made-up face twitched. "Raccoons?" he said. "On a tray?"

"And was one of them wearing... you know?"

"Pants," continued Raymond. "And the other one had a hat. Yes," he said, staring into space. "That's what raccoons wear round here. I've seen them everywhere. They sometimes take pictures…" he said, his voice trailing away.

The car continued on its journey, the men in silent contemplation.

The raccoons landed with a thump. They were zipping down the mountain, but the jump had veered them off course. "Hard right!" ordered Quickpaw and four furry bodies leant so hard their ears almost touched the snow.

"Looks like the trucks have beaten us," said Rocky, daring to raise a paw and point towards the village. The four vehicles had pulled up outside Max's General Store and the men were getting out.

"We're not beaten yet," squealed Quickpaw, using his paws like paddles, coaxing the tray to maximum speed. "We have to get to Max before it's too late."

CHAPTER 12

Faking It

It was early and Max sat outside in the fresh morning air. The old man was deep in thought. He looked at his boarded-up windows and then down the street at all the 'Sold' signs. He'd seen plenty of good times, but this definitely rated as his worst. The rampaging bear story was global news. Bookings at the local hotel were zero. Trade was non-existent. Raymond had pleaded with him at last night's meeting. "You've been offered a good price, Unc," he'd explained. "It's crazy not to sell."

Max watched the sun rise over the mountain and rocked himself in his chair. "Then maybe I'm a crazy old fool," muttered the old man under his breath. He watched as four cars wound down the mountainside. They made it to the village and Max was surprised when they pulled up outside his store. He recognised the man in the suit and touched the brim of his cap in a 'good morning' gesture. Raymond fell out of the lead vehicle. He'd spilt half a bottle of fake blood on to his trousers and dabbed a bit round his fake neck wound. The snow turned red. Max creaked his knees upright as his nephew crawled towards the steps.

"Bears," he whimpered, collapsing in a heap. "Killer bears!"

The posse of men jumped out of the cars and helped Raymond to his feet. His shirt was ripped and the gash on his neck was particularly gory. "We've called an ambulance," shouted one of the baddies, looking as concerned as he could. "We found this man in the woods."

"Bears," moaned Raymond again. "Hundreds of them. A swarm!"

One of the men aimed a sharp heel into Raymond's foot, causing him to yelp for real. "Don't overdo it, sonny," he snarled under his breath. Max recognised his battered and bruised nephew and came down the steps to help. The baddies allowed Max to help carry the wounded man on to the wooden stoop where they laid him on a couch.

"Grizzlies, Unc, "he whimpered in an almost dying breath. "You must sell up and leave. Or you might..." Raymond's eyes flickered dramatically, like he'd seen on the television, "...die," he said softly, his eyes closing.

One of the baddies looked at Uncle Max and shook his head. "I'm sorry, sir," he said. "The ambulance is on its way, but he sure is badly mauled."

The raccoons were nearly at the bottom of the mountain. "Hard left!" yelled Quickpaw as the first of the houses loomed into view. The team lurched and the tea tray sped through a snowy garden.

"There's a fence ahead!" yelled Rocky, peeping from behind Sunshine's hat. "How are we going to stop?"

Quickpaw wasn't sure they could. He

saw an open gate and went for it. "Left again," he barked and the tray bolted through the gap and continued down the slope. There were houses ahead and the tray was showing no signs of slowing. "Brakes on!" yelled the leader, demonstrating by jamming his back paws into the snow. Eight raccoon feet ploughed into the snow and the tray slowed a little.

"Still too fast," yelled Rocky as they sped towards Mrs Grady's farm. Quickpaw spotted an opportunity and lurched his friends sharp right. The speeding tea tray shot through Mrs Grady's open barn door. The snow ran out and the tray screeched across the concrete floor, sparks flying. The raccoons ducked as the tray sped under a cow and out through another door, back into the snow. They were now on the high street. Max's General Store was just a hundred metres down the hill. But time was running out.

Max was devastated. His nephew lay unconscious on the couch. The old man paced nervously up and down, biting his lip. "This is awful. Another bear attack. What if he dies?"

"Then I'm afraid we'd have to withdraw our very generous offer," said the man in the suit. "Look here, Max. We admire your attitude. But, quite frankly, if Raymond dies from this savage and unprovoked bear attack, the village is finished. And your stubbornness will cost you everything."

Another of the men shuffled in with a briefcase and pulled out some papers. He handed them to Max. "Our original offer still stands," he said. "And looking at the state of your nephew, it is now a very generous offer indeed."

Max looked at his nephew's wounds. Raymond managed a dramatic flicker of his eyelids. "That grizzly's done me good and proper," he croaked. "Don't let him mess you up too."

Max was white with fear. He could be about to lose his nephew and his shop. The man laid the papers out in front of the old man and handed him a pen.

Raymond issued a pained groan for effect. "Grizzlies," he whimpered.

Max looked at his nephew. The wound on his neck looked awful. He picked up the pen and his eyes scanned the document.

"Just sign," growled the suited man, unable to contain his irritation.

Max's hand was shaking as he placed the pen on the paper. A strange noise filled the early morning air. Max looked up the high street and did a double take.

He dropped the pen and rubbed his eyes.
"What the heck?" he began.

A tray of raccoons was speeding down the snowy street. One was waving. One was wearing a cowboy hat and another seemed to be wearing Superman pants. Max saw eight raccoon legs jamming into the dirty snow.

Sunshine raised his hat to Max as he came into view. Quickpaw pointed a paw at some bales of hay. The four raccoons leant left and assumed the crash position as the home-made sledge smashed into the bales.

and he beamed. "Ripped my pants, but otherwise OK," he reported, showing his friends a huge tear across his backside.

They located Quickpaw, face down in the mud. Sunshine rolled him over. His eyes were closed and blood trickled from his mouth. "He took the full force," sobbed Rocky. "He's a hero."

Quickpaw wearily opened an eye. "Ouch," he groaned. His friends helped him to his feet and he stood shakily.

were going, it co~~ ~~

worse!"

Quickpaw grinned, showing a huge gap in his teeth. "Battered and bruised," he said, "but we've delivered our evidence."

"Am I alive?" croaked Rocky.

"I can hear you so you must be," smiled Dempsey, sitting up in the straw and handing Sunshine his hat.

Rocky's face peeped. He looked at the raccoons inquisitively, picking it up and brushing off the mud.

Max pressed a button and the camera sprang into life. He looked at Rocky and recognised the underwear. "The Hole-in-the-Tree gang?" he muttered, looking at the animals and then down at the camera. He saw a picture of Raymond holding a huge pair of bear shoes. He clicked again and there was a scene showing his nephew diving into the lake. "And not

a bear in sight," noticed the shopkeeper,

his brow furrowed. A few more clicks took

him to a close-up of an oil refinery and a

lady applying make-up to Raymond. He

looked up at the men, his brow furrowed. He glanced down at the camera and the pieces began to slot into place.

Max stomped up the stairs to his dying nephew. "Raymond," he yelled, throwing a glass of cold water in the young man's face.

"Cripes, Uncle Max," wailed his nephew, sitting bolt upright. "What ya do that for?"

"Waking you from your deathbed," snapped Max. He poked a finger into Raymond's neck wound. "This isn't blood…" he said, looking up angrily.

"Y—you don't understand," stammered Raymond.

"Oh, but I do understand," bellowed Max. "This little sales scam isn't about wild animals. More like wild criminals!" he yelled, wafting his hands at the men. "My sister said you were a waster. Bad news. But it had always been petty crime. Well, nephew, this is a major crime. And you are going to pay a very heavy price indeed."

Dozens of villagers had heard the commotion and a small crowd had gathered. Max waved the paperwork in the air. "We've been conned!" he yelled. "These men aren't going to build an eco-village. And there's no bear. They're greedy businessmen who are going to turn our village into an oil well." The old man was shaking with anger as he ripped the contract in two. "And I suggest you do the same," he shouted.

The conmen were surrounded and the villagers held the criminal gang until a police van turned up. The men were handcuffed and led away.

The raccoons stood on Max's roof and watched. Raymond looked up as the van pulled away. He saw four raccoons. One was waving. Another had his paws in his ears, wiggling his fingers at the men. He was sure one of the raccoons was pointing a camera at him. The flash temporarily blinded him. Raymond was handcuffed so

he couldn't rub his eyes. Instead he looked away and did an extra-large blink. He looked back at the window and one of the raccoons was smacking its underpanted

bottom and blowing kisses. Raymond decided that, once in prison, he would seek some therapy.

CHAPTER 13

Inside Job

The snow had melted. The villagers had worked hard to clean up the sludge. The dam was repaired, the 'For Sale' signs gone and village life was back to normal. It was mid-morning as the gang shimmied down their tree.

"You sure we should be doing this?" asked Rocky, tugging at his pants. "We're on good terms with Max. It seems risky."

"Risky is letting our food stocks run down to zero," argued Quickpaw. "Risky is when a raccoon becomes too relaxed. So we need to go with Sunshine's plan."

Sunshine stood upright, like he'd seen outlaws do on the television. He cracked his knuckles. "This little raccoon prides himself on breaking and entering. Nowhere is off limits. That's why we're going to have another go at Max's high security storeroom." He lifted his hat to reveal a small hacksaw. "Expect the unexpected," he reminded them.

A toothless grin lit up Quickpaw's lips. "I've got to hand it to you, dude," he said. "You absolutely never give up."

The raccoons scampered through the forest to the edge of the village. It was buzzing with people and traffic. They sat in the shadows and watched the world go by. Sunshine looked up at the sun.

"Anytime now," he said, "there will be a delivery van at Max's. Same time every day."

Right on cue a van chugged down the street and pulled up outside Max's General Store. The driver unlocked the back of his truck and shuffled three large boxes on to the pavement. "Stock," explained Sunshine. "For the storeroom."

Sunshine knew exactly what was going to happen next. His friends watched, rather puzzled, as the man lifted one of the heavy boxes and staggered inside to find the shopkeeper.

"I don't get it," hissed Rocky. "What's the plan?"

"Midnight," yapped Sunshine. "Back here. I'll need some help shifting a massive load of food." Sunshine waited for a gap in the traffic before calmly scampering across the road and nosing his way into one of the boxes. He sank inside just as the delivery man came out and grabbed the box. He heaved it into the store.

"He's been captured!" said Dempsey.

"Given himself up," suggested Rocky. "I don't get it!"

The three remaining raccoons scampered across the road. Quickpaw stood on Dempsey's shoulders and peered into Max's shop window. Max had signed for the delivery and was lugging Sunshine's box towards the storeroom. He put the box down and fumbled for the key. With Max's back turned, Sunshine poked his head out of the box and tipped the brim of his hat towards Quickpaw. The raccoon leader saluted him. Then Sunshine bobbed back inside the box and Max pushed him into the storeroom and locked the door.

"W—what's happening?" stammered Dempsey. "Is it another raid?"

Quickpaw grinned. "Sure is, buddy," he said. "And this one's an inside job."

Awesome adventures with the wildest wildlife!

OUT NOW!